A DOG NAMED FROG

BY
CHRISTINE J IVY

COPYRIGHTS

COPYRIGHT © 2024 BY CHRISTINE J IVY.

ALL RIGHTS RESERVED. NO PART OF THIS BOOK, INCLUDING THE ILLUSTRATIONS, MAY BE REPRODUCED IN ANY FORM OR BY ANY ELECTRONIC OR MECHANICAL MEANS, INCLUDING INFORMATION STORAGE AND RETRIEVAL SYSTEMS, WITHOUT PRIOR PERMISSION IN WRITING FROM THE AUTHOR, EXCEPT BY REVIEWERS WHO MAY QUOTE BRIEF PASSAGES IN A REVIEW.

THIS PUBLICATION CONTAINS THE OPINIONS, IDEAS, AND CREATIVE ILLUSTRATIONS OF ITS AUTHOR. IT IS INTENDED TO PROVIDE HELPFUL AND INFORMATIVE MATERIAL ON THE SUBJECTS ADDRESSED. THE AUTHOR AND PUBLISHER DISCLAIM ALL RESPONSIBILITY FOR ANY LIABILITY, LOSS, OR RISK—PERSONAL OR OTHERWISE—INCURRED AS A CONSEQUENCE, DIRECTLY OR INDIRECTLY, OF THE USE AND APPLICATION OF ANY OF THE CONTENTS OR ILLUSTRATIONS IN THIS BOOK.

ISBN: 978-1-966131-01-4

AUTHOR BIO

MY NAME IS CHRISTINE IVY AND I HAVE WORKED IN EDUCATION FOR OVER 20 YEARS. I AM MARRIED AND HAVE TWO BOYS AND FOUR GRANDCHILDREN. CHILDREN HAVE INSPIRED ME IN SO MANY WAYS AND THAT IS WHY I WROTE THIS BOOK. THERE IS NO ONE SIZE FITS ALL WHEN IT COMES TO LEARNING. I WROTE THIS IN THE HOPE THAT IT WILL INSPIRE AND TEACH. AFTERALL EDUCATION IS THE ONE THING IN THIS WORLD THAT NOBODY CAN TAKE AWAY FROM YOU. I HOPE YOU ENJOY READING IT AS MUCH AS I DID WRITING IT.

ACKNOWLEDGMENTS

I WANT TO THANK MY FRIENDS AND FAMILY FOR THEIR SUPPORT AND VERY SPECIAL THANK YOU TO MY BEST FRIEND LISA SILVA FOR BELIEVING IN ME. I ALSO WANT TO THANK SEAN DONOVAN FOR ALL HIS HELP!

DEDICATION

I WANT TO DEDICATE THIS BOOK TO MY GRANDCHILDREN: LANDON, JAXSYN, SKARLETTE AND PRESTYN

Down a country road, there lived this little old man named Harry. Harry adopted a little puppy with a lot of energy.

Harry said to his new little buddy, "You sure do jump around a lot. I think I should just call you Frog." The dog jumped up and down, and Harry said, "So Frog it is!"

Frog was just so happy to have a home and to be out in the country. Frog loved his new human friend, Harry and his forever home. The feelings were mutual. Harry had been alone for a while and wanted a companion.

Frog was so happy he started jumping up and down and all around. Soon, Frog was jumping over logs. Harry was so happy with the dog he named Frog.

Frog wanted to explore his new surroundings, so with his nose to the ground and his tail wagging, it wasn't long before Frog met his first new friend, a real frog.

"Hi, my name is Frog; may I ask what your name is?" The frog responded, "My name is Kitty."

"Nice to meet you Kitty!"

"Frog was so pleased to have a new friend. He asked Kitty if she wanted to go exploring with him, and she was excited too and said, "Sure!"

So, Frog the dog and Kitty the frog ventured on their way as they talked, walked, jumped and hopped. The two liked playing and exploring together.

Frog and Kitty both enjoyed their newfound friendship. They ventured on and met a little gray and white kitty. Kitty the frog greeted the furry little thing and asked him his name. He said, "My name is Squirrel."

Frog and Kitty both welcomed Squirrel. They explained how they were just exploring and asked Squirrel if he would like to join them. He said, "Sure, that sounds like fun!"

So, Frog the dog, Kitty the frog, and Squirrel the kitty continued on their way, jumping, hopping and skipping down the beaten path. They saw flowers, butterflies and a few bugs. There was a pond and, of course, trees.

Venturing on, they come to a tree and Frog, the dog, felt something hit him on the head. He looked up and there was a squirrel in a Walnut Tree. The squirrel was a cute little critter with a fluffy tail and a little patch of fur sticking up on his head.

The squirrel apologized to Frog, the dog about the walnut incident. Frog introduced himself, and the frog named Kitty and the Kitty named Squirrel. Squirrel said, "Nice to meet all of you." "My name is Rooster."

"My mom picked my name because of the hair sticking up on my head."

"No worries," said Frog. "We are all out just exploring. Would you like to come along?"

"I certainly would," said Rooster. Thank you for inviting me!"

So as Frog, Kitty, Squirrel and Rooster continued on the beaten path without a care in the world, they were led to an open green pasture. In the pasture stood a huge, brown cow. They all greeted the cow with enthusiasm. "By the way, my name is Moose, and it is really nice to meet all of you!"

Kitty asked Moose if he would like to go exploring with them. Moose was delighted by the invite and accepted kindly. Moose was always sure to mind his manners. He was such a big fellow that he was afraid he would scare others off.

So as Frog the dog, Kitty the frog, Squirrel the Kitty, a Squirrel named Rooster and the cow named Moose walked, hopped, skipped and jumped. They chatted and enjoyed the beautiful countryside as well as their new friend. It was a breath of fresh air, literally.

Up ahead was a huge grove of trees. The group of friends looked around at each other, and it was unanimous that they were going to explore the woods.

Before long, the entourage of friends, who looked like a parade of animals that escaped a petting zoo, came upon a character that made Moose, the cow, look like a typical cow.

With all of their eyes beaming in awe there stood in front of them an actual Moose in all its splendor. He stood tall, with a big chest and a full rack of antlers on his head. He looked like a king!

The handsome creature turned his head and was in as much awe as they were. The friends came upon a real Moose. "Hello there," said the moose, "Well, hello," they all said.

They introduced themselves one by one. The moose said, "My name is Fox."

Fox asked the group, what brings them to his neck of the woods? The squirrel, named Rooster, looked up at the majestic animal and said, "We are being adventurous and just exploring." "Would you like to join us?"

"Sure, why not?" replied Fox, the moose.

They let Fox lead the way since they were all a little far from home and had no idea how to navigate the wooded area. They noticed a variety of birds up in the trees, leafy foliage, a few wildflowers and an obvious trail that Fox made himself.

As they followed Fox on the trail, they came to something that looked like a den. Out of the den came a real fox. The moose named Fox said, "Hello, Harry!" Harry was a Fox and a friend of Fox's already.

Fox turned to everyone and said, "This is my friend Harry." All of a sudden, Frog the dog panicked and said loudly, "Harry!" "Harry is my human and he must be filled with worry, wondering where I went off to!"

Harry the fox said, "I could surely walk back with all of you to make sure you get home safely."

"That is very kind of you," said Frog the dog. "It would be greatly appreciated. Thank you."

Leaving behind the Moose named Fox, all of the friends said their goodbyes and followed Harry out of the woods as he walked side by side with Frog the dog. Along the way, as they dropped their newfound friends off one by one, Frog and Harry talked.

Frog and Harry had a lot in common. They became very fast friends and enjoyed many of the same activities. Frog asked Harry the Fox if he would like to go exploring with him sometime. Harry said, "Sure, that would be great!"

It really doesn't matter what you look like, what your name is, where you come from or even what language you speak; nothing says more or speaks louder than acceptance and kindness.